I Will Paint You *Another Sky*

Deborah Wagner Brenneman

WestBow Press books may be ordered through booksellers or by contacting:

WestBow Press
A Division of Thomas Nelson & Zondervan
1663 Liberty Drive
Bloomington, IN 47403
www.westbowpress.com
844-714-3454

Interior Image Credit: Danielle Brennan

ISBN: 979-8-3850-3797-1 (sc)
ISBN: 979-8-3850-3798-8 (hc)
ISBN: 979-8-3850-3796-4 (e)

Library of Congress Control Number: 2024923874

Print information available on the last page.

WestBow Press rev. date: 02/22/2025

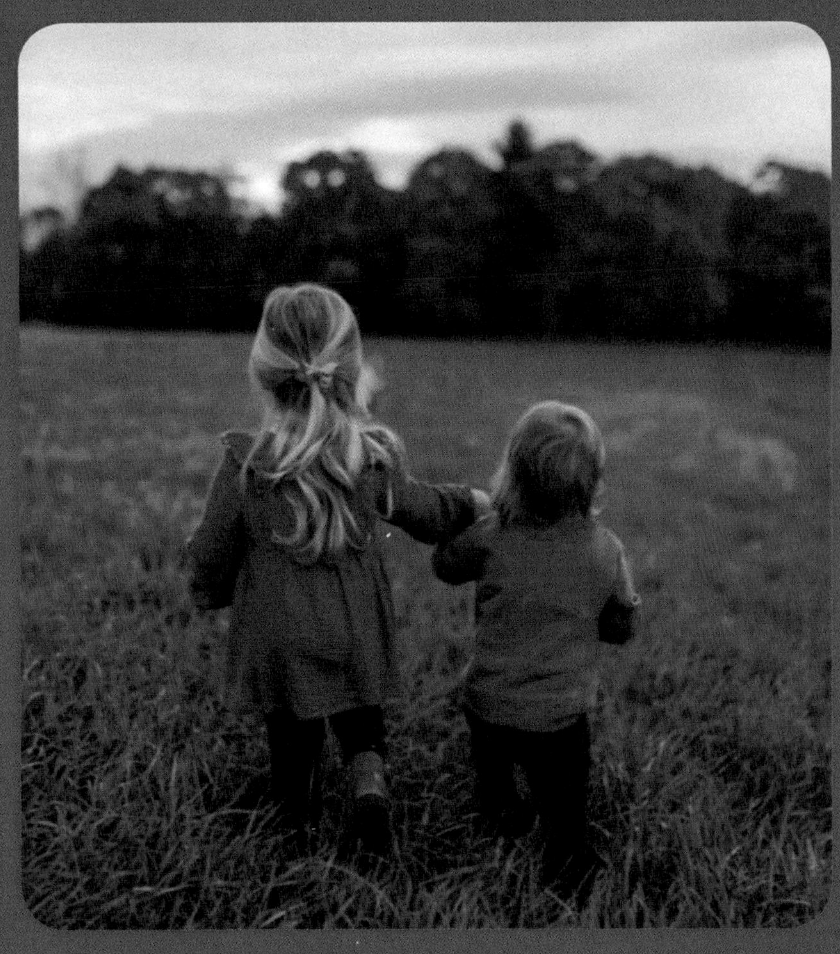

Genesis 1:6-8

And God said, “Let there be an expanse between the waters to separate water from water.” So God made the expanse and separated the water under the expanse from the water above it. And it was so. God called the expanse “sky.” And there was evening, and there was morning-the second day.

Dedication

This book is dedicated to my sister, Jeanie. We will never forget your courageous battle of fighting cancer and the life lessons you taught all of us through your journey.

It is also dedicated to all of you fighting cancer.
We are praying for a cure and healing.

Kathy Z. Thank you!! You are wonderful!!

On the day you were born
the sky was as blue and clear
as your eyes. I was by your
side and we began to discover
an entire world that revealed
itself through the sky.

You could see for miles the beautiful world you came into. You were curious and loved the life God had blessed you with.

You and I would lie on the green grass and watch the soft white clouds glide by. You pretended the inflatable clouds were your friends and you blew kisses to them as they floated past us.

The soft happy clouds began to move upward and they began to fill up with the color gray. You thought the clouds were getting mad. We can feel anger and sadness at times, just like the clouds.

The beautiful fluffy clouds had disappeared. Your eyes became bigger as you watched the clouds change. You asked, “Will my friends change like the clouds? Will they become angry at me? And will I become sad?”

"They may," I replied. "Sometimes our friends will say bad things about us or cause us to feel lonely. We want to hold onto them, but just like the clouds, we need to watch them go away. There will be brighter days coming. I will paint you another sky."

The wind began to blow and the clouds formed an anvil and pointed in the direction the storm was coming. We quickly ran inside our home and looked at the sky from our window. Rain began to fall and lightning bolts streaked across the sky.

The storm didn't last long. But, long enough for us to snuggle and for you to understand that I promise to be by your side.

God's promise is sealed with a rainbow, my promise is sealed with a kiss! You will learn as you grow, whom you can trust and whom you cannot. And I will be by your side on the sunny days as well as the days filled with storms. "I will paint you another sky."

The sky returned to a beautiful blue once the storm had passed. A few happy clouds returned.

The warmth of the sun remained and the showers brought rising steam from the ground. We stepped back outside and our feet became wet as we walked through the grass.

We walked to a place where we watched the clouds form above us in the bright blue sky. We placed a blanket on the ground but weren't really worried about getting wet. The clouds were thinning and appeared wispy. The wind gently moved them.

"I will paint you another sky."

You tell me the clouds are beautiful and I agree. We lie silently holding hands, listening and watching. The sky is a canvas that God paints every day. Each cloud is perfectly formed by His brush.

The day is coming to a close. Evening and night will soon be here. The clouds begin to mask themselves as the sun is setting. You can see the sun's light as it slips behind the horizon.

The sun disappears and the moon shows itself. The clouds surround the shining moon. I am by your side and we decide to walk home. One day you will lie on the grass with your own children and tell them about the clouds. You will tell them of the different types and you will share the stories I have told you.

You will share that there is happiness in life and also storms we will go through. Tell them how much you love them and how you will be by their side. Near or far, "I will paint you another sky. I promise."

Printed in the United States
by Baker & Taylor Publisher Services